Mel ran a finger round the back of her collar. She felt unbearably hot. And now that she'd noticed it, the classroom itself was suddenly stifling. No movement stirred the air. It was like the hottest of summer days. Yet outside the rain poured down and gusts of wind blew leaves around the playground.

Mel went on singing, as if in a trance, but as she did so, she felt a tightening in the back of her throat. Suddenly it was difficult to breathe. Then she realized why. A faint haze of chalk dust hung in the air. She could see the tiny particles dancing before her eyes. But where had it come from?

Then she caught sight of the blackboard... a message was appearing in the chalk dust. A message written in spidery capitals. A message written by an unseen hand.

**Other titles in this series
coming soon...**

Letters from the Grave

Felicity Everett

First published in 1996 by Usborne Publishing Ltd,
Usborne House, 83-85 Saffron Hill,
London EC1N 8RT, England.

ISBN 0 7460 2476 2 (paperback)
ISBN 0 7460 2477 0 (hardback)

Typeset in Palatino
Printed in Great Britain

Series Editor: Gaby Waters
Editor: Phil Roxbee Cox
Designer: Lucy Parris
Cover illustration: Barry Jones

CONTENTS

1

She thinks she's so clever

"Well she certainly stands out from the crowd!" whispered Stevely Barraclough to her friend Mel, as a new girl walked into the classroom. "She must be the Kate Thackery we've heard *so* much about. Yawn!"

It was three weeks into the Autumn Term when Kate joined Cecily Fane High School, so she was bound to be the target for Stevely's attentions.

Mel giggled nervously. Kate did look weird. With her pale skin, hollow cheeks and frizzy ginger hair, she drew their eyes like a magnet.

She was tall, gawky and too big for her second-hand school uniform, which she wore with a prim and proper air; more like a dummy in the school outfitter's shop window, than a real live human being.

And then there were her eyes. They were light grey, almost unnaturally pale which made them seem ice-cold. And she had a piercing stare that was strangely unsettling.

It was a fairly safe bet that Stevely meant her remark about Kate to be nasty, but with Stevely you could never be certain. And, if Mel jumped to the wrong conclusion and said the wrong thing, Stevely was quite capable of cutting her down to size with a sarcastic remark... even though Mel was supposed to be part of her inner circle of friends.

Mel decided that it was best to keep quiet, until she was absolutely sure what Stevely meant. As it turned out, it was Kate Thackery's hair that had caught Stevely's eye.

Mel couldn't help feeling a little sorry for Kate. It wasn't at all desirable to come to the attention of Stevely Barraclough for the wrong reasons. Stevely had influence. It wasn't that she was well-liked exactly, although many of her classmates – especially the boys – appreciated her sarcastic humour. No. Stevely was respected, feared even.

If you weren't actually part of Stevely's gang, it

was best either to go along with what she wanted, or melt into the background. Otherwise Stevely could make life quite unpleasant for you. As Kate Thackery was about to find out.

Kate had moved to Cecily Fane High from a private girls' school in the country. According to the rumours, she'd had a luxurious lifestyle, a large house with a swimming pool and even a pony of her own. Until her dad lost his job. Then they'd had to move in with Kate's ancient aunt, on the wrong side of Groombridge. At least that's what the rumours said when Kate *first* arrived, but school rumours often change and grow.

Anyway, Kate was a new kid who probably thought that she was better than anyone else. As far as Stevely was concerned, this made her fair game for a little 'attention'.

To start with it was pretty routine stuff – the kind of teasing and mickey-taking most newcomers have to put up with.

"Which way is the toilet?" Kate asked Stevely at break on her first morning at her new school.

"Go to the end of the corridor, turn left and it's the door opposite the Staff Room," replied Stevely, winking at her friends as Kate walked away. "It sometimes sticks, so push really hard."

"You've just sent her to the *staff* toilet," pointed

3

out Tony, unnecessarily.

They could already hear the furious tones of Miss Cawley ringing out from down the corridor.

"You impertinent girl, what makes you think you can barge in here like this? This wash-room is out of bounds to pupils."

"Well, she never said which toilet she meant," said Stevely shrugging her shoulders in mock innocence.

In French later that morning, Kate answered three questions faultlessly, in a brilliant French accent. Mademoiselle Papin was so impressed that she forgot herself for ten minutes and the two of them carried on a fluent conversation about French seaside resorts.

The rest of the class sat gawping at them as if they were from another planet.

"She thinks she's so clever," sneered Stevely, with more than a hint of jealousy. Mel could tell that she was really rattled. Stevely didn't like not knowing what was going on. If there was one thing she hated more than know-alls, it was feeling left out. So at lunchtime, Stevely decided to give Kate a taste of her own medicine.

"Pangyou losay frightish new girlus?" she said to Mel, as they queued behind Kate in the school canteen.

"You what?" said Mel, looking blank. Stevely jerked her head in Kate's direction and gave Mel a look that said 'play along'.

"Yah, mishtish snobby fruitcakee," Mel replied, making up the words as she went.

"Bendelishdish uglimugosa et tres big-headed n'est-ce pas?" put in Jason, eager to show off his new-found gift for languages.

By now Kate was in no doubt who they were talking about. The gang kept it up until she had gone to sit in the furthest corner of the canteen at a table by herself. Even then, Stevely's crowd kept looking over at her and laughing.

Mel felt a twinge of pity, but then she reminded herself what a show-off Kate had been in French. She deserved it. Stuck-up swot.

Kate's slate grey eyes met Mel's across the room. Mel shuddered as the new girl's piercing stare held her gaze as though she could read Mel's mind. It was all Mel could do to drag her eyes away and return to her half-eaten yoghurt.

2

Strange, but true

That afternoon, when Kate Thackery found herself between lessons with no idea where she was supposed to go next, she knew better than to ask Stevely. Instead, she asked a nervous blonde girl called Jane Geary.

Jane didn't belong to Stevely's group. She was a bit of a loner. She was one of those people who liked to do things her own way, but wouldn't give Stevely any trouble. Unfortunately for Kate, however, Stevely had overheard.

"It's History next. In Room Seven. Next to the Library. Isn't it, Jane?"

Jane didn't answer, she just took the stairs two at a time to get out of Stevely's way.

Mr. Bennett, the history teacher, was no pushover. Even Stevely sat up and took notice when Mr. Bennett was in one of his moods, and from the way he stalked into the classroom today, it looked like being one of those days.

"Right 8C. Ivan the Terrible. Who was he?" he barked, throwing last week's history tests down on his desk in an untidy heap.

"8C's history teacher," murmured Jason under his breath, causing a ripple of amusement in the class. Poor Jason.

"Stand up, Taylor," Mr. Bennett said to Jason in a quiet, menacing voice. "I didn't quite catch what you said. Would you mind repeating it for the benefit of the class?"

Jason shifted uneasily from foot to foot.

"Nothing, sir."

"Come on, boy. It can't have been nothing. Your classmates clearly found it highly amusing. WHAT DID YOU SAY?"

It was at this moment that Kate came into the room, apologising for being late. She made no mention of having been deliberately sent to the wrong classroom. The rest of the class held its breath.

Mr. Bennett's face switched from a look of fury, to one of false politeness and concern. "I do beg your pardon, miss. We seem to have started without you. You must forgive our rudeness in not waiting five minutes to see whether we could accommodate any latecomers."

Not knowing Mr. Bennett, Kate's face relaxed into a smile. She didn't notice several class members wincing as she started to say: "Oh, I quite underst..."

"HOW DARE YOU WALTZ INTO MY CLASSROOM FIVE MINUTES LATE AND TELL ME YOU QUITE UNDERSTAND! WHO DO YOU THINK YOU ARE?" Mr. Bennett unleashed a double dose of anger, Jason's share as well as her own, on poor unsuspecting Kate.

She kept opening her mouth to say 'sorry', but Mr. Bennett just went on and on, getting more and more angry and sarcastic, until Kate's strange, grey eyes seemed to burn with the injustice of what was happening to her. Mel wouldn't have blamed her if she'd burst into tears... but that obviously wasn't Kate's way.

As she watched Kate getting told off, Stevely had a look of smug satisfaction on her face.

Mel looked away in embarrassment. The room suddenly seemed cold... very cold. She could feel goose pimples rising on the back of her neck, yet she still had her blazer on, and all the doors and windows were shut tight.

Then, out of the corner of her eye, Mel noticed a movement on Mr. Bennett's desk. It was barely there, yet noticeable all the same.

There it was again! The pile of test papers that the teacher had thrown down when he came into the classroom rustled gently. It was as though they were stirred by a slight breeze.

Mel found herself shuddering again. What was the big deal about some rustling papers? Why did it bother her so much? But, somehow, it *did*.

Forgetting the sideshow of Mr. Bennett and Kate, Mel stared in puzzled fascination at the moving papers. Before her eyes, the rustling was becoming a fluttering and soon the papers were flapping wildly as though whipped by a force ten gale – in a room without so much as a draught.

"And if this happens again... " Mr. Bennett was saying, bright red in the face now, and his voice beginning to crack from the strain of shouting.

Suddenly, he realized that Kate was the only one listening to him. The attention of the rest of the class seemed to be elsewhere.

Now that he had stopped yelling, Mr. Bennett couldn't fail to notice the disturbance. He rubbed his upper arms briskly as the chill in the atmosphere struck him for the first time.

He was about to turn his anger on whoever had the cheek to interfere with the test papers, when he realized that no one was anywhere near them.

The desk and the papers stood alone.

By now, the desk itself had started to shake, gently at first, and then more and more violently. Its lid rattled like a loose shutter banging in a storm and, as the class watched in disbelief, the whole thing began bucking from side to side, as though... as though it were alive.

Mel looked wildly around the class, wondering if this was what an earthquake felt like, but it was a strange earthquake which only affected one piece of furniture in the whole room. Everything else was quite still. A bead of sweat trickled down the back of her neck.

Just when it seemed as if the rattling desk might fall over, the papers rose, as if sucked up by a small tornado. They whirled around in the air for a moment, with a weird humming noise that made Mel's ears sing. Then they flew across the classroom one by one, *as if flung by an unseen hand*... straight into the astonished face of Stevely Barraclough.

Stevely leapt up, as though a swarm of bees was attacking her. She flapped her arms and squealed hysterically, but no one came to her aid.

Everyone was frozen by a mixture of strange fascination and fear. Mel sat rooted to the spot, like an animal mesmerized by the lights of an oncoming car.

It wasn't until the last sheet of paper had fluttered to the ground, and Stevely had fallen to the floor, that the spell was broken and everyone started talking at once.

"What on earth..?"

"That's the weirdest thing ever."

"Did you see that?"

"Are you OK, Stevely?" Mel put her arm around Stevely's shoulders, a little nervously, but Stevely shook it off.

"Of course I'm OK," she said, "It was just a rickety old desk and a gust of wind, that's all. You don't think it's going to give me sleepless nights do you?" But Mel knew Stevely well enough to tell that she'd been frightened, like the rest of them.

Mr. Bennett decided that the strange disturbance must *somehow* have been an ingenious practical joke and made the whole class stay on after home-time. They had to sit in the classroom for an hour but, when no one would own up to the 'childish prank', he finally dismissed them.

The class saw the whole incident very differently.

After a while, talk turned to supernatural powers... to poltergeists... and to strange force fields. Everyone was filled with a heady mixture of excitement and the fear of the unknown. What had happened back there?

It was Jason Taylor who brought them down to earth with a bump. "If someone in 8C *does* have supernatural powers, I wish they'd transport Mr. Bennett to a teachers' retirement home," he said. "Why waste them on a pile of papers?"

His classmates laughed, but it was hollow laughter. Kate Thackery's first day at Cecily Fane High had certainly been a strange one, but no one could have guessed what was yet to come.

3

Enemies

"She's not actually that bad, you know," Matt told Mel as the two friends filed into the drama studio the following week.

"Who isn't?"

"Kate. I got talking to her on the way home from school the other day. Okay she's a bit different, but she's into some interesting things."

"Oh, yes?" said Mel, rolling her eyes in the way she'd seen Stevely do. "French conversation, table manners, flower arranging, basket weaving?"

"Don't be silly," said Matt, sounding exasperated. "I mean she likes sci-fi movies, virtual reality, music..."

Mel looked doubtful. "It's the way she *looks* that freaks me out," she said. "She's so pale, with those big grey eyes. She's like some... " she paused, choosing her words with care. "...like some living dummy."

"Well, we can't all look like supermodels," smirked Matt. Mel laughed sheepishly. She wasn't exactly catwalk material herself, it was true, but at least she fitted in.

"Supermodels?" said Stevely, who had just walked into the drama studio. "Are you talking about me again, Matt?"

"He was just saying how well he's been getting on with Kate," said Mel.

An irritated frown flitted across Stevely's face. She immediately masked it by putting on a soppy, doggy-eyed expression and pretending to be a lovelorn Matt.

"Oh Kate, my darling, lovely Kate!" crooned Stevely, going down on one knee and clasping both hands over her heart dramatically. Most of the class had noticed her act by now. People were laughing and nudging each other and Matt was blushing furiously.

Kate was standing a little way away, pretending to study the noticeboard, but Mel could tell from the way that she narrowed her eyes that she had been watching and listening to Stevely.

Mel felt a stab of guilt that she had caused this latest outburst by telling Stevely what Matt had said. A stab of guilt... and the slightest trace of fear.

Mel was unnerved by Kate's coolness – by her coldness. Kate wasn't reacting in the way she was supposed to react. She was *supposed* to be upset, or annoyed or to fight back, not simply to be there, unmoved... listening, watching, staring.

The rest of that week passed without any more awkward scenes. Life at Cecily Fane High carried on pretty much as normal. Kate quietly got on with her lessons. She seemed to be an ordinary schoolgirl when she was with the few people who were nice to her – totally different from the chilling figure she became when Stevely was taunting her.

But in the last lesson on Friday, which was Chemistry, Kate made the mistake of putting up her hand to answer a question.

"Yes, you, the new girl. Don't be shy. I won't bite you if you get it wrong," said Miss Goodall, the science teacher.

"Lead," said Kate.

"Quite right, dear. The chemical represented by the letters 'Pb' is lead." She beamed at Kate encouragingly. "You'd better watch out, 8C, it seems your new classmate is a step ahead of you. Not that being a step ahead of you lot makes her a genius, mind you."

"No, but she thinks it does," muttered Stevely.

Towards the end of the lesson, just as they were tidying up after an experiment, Miss Goodall was called away on an urgent errand.

"Jane, you take charge please, I know I can trust you to be sensible. When I get back, I expect to find the lab clean and tidy and all of you quietly writing up your results. No one – I repeat, *no one* – is to touch any of the chemicals or equipment except for what you're putting away. Clear?"

The class mumbled a half-hearted response. Jane Geary walked up to the teacher's desk as if Miss Goodall had asked her to walk the plank.

Stevely grinned. Kate was about to find out what being her enemy really meant.

4

Getting warmer

"Now we'll have some fun," said Stevely. Mel's heart sank. Stevely hadn't got tired of baiting Kate. She'd just been biding her time – waiting for the right moment to attack.

Stevely picked up a test-tube from the work bench beside her. A mischievous smile played around her lips.

Stevely was planning something. Mel knew it. Sending Kate to the wrong room or using words against her didn't seem to be having any effect. Kate Thackery was proving to be a hard nut to crack. There was something weird about her as well, the way she refused to respond to Stevely's taunts, and those cool, staring eyes.

Stevely added a few drops of tap water to the sticky black chemical in the bottom of the test-tube and shook it, experimentally. She smirked at the evil-looking mess, then met Kate's gaze with a cold smile. Stevely would show her who was Number One around here.

"That's a nice white shirt you're wearing, Kate," she said, menacingly. "Wouldn't it be a shame if you got it dirty? I bet Mumsie would be very angry with little Katie!" She took a step towards her intended victim.

The wide aisle which separated Stevely and Kate had emptied. Abandoned lab stools littered Stevely's route, where her classmates had drifted, as casually as they could, out of the line of fire.

Now they flanked the work benches on either side, eager to watch from a safe distance and thankful that they weren't the target of Stevely's attentions.

Glass flasks and metal tongs lay abandoned all around. Here and there a tap dripped into a gleaming ceramic sink. Pairs of lifeless Bunsen burners lined either side of Stevely's path, like candlesticks decorating the nave of a church.

She took a step towards Kate, rolling the test-tube playfully between her thumb and forefinger.

"Come on Stevely, put it down," said Jane Geary, in what she meant to be a brisk, friendly voice, but which came out as a strangled squeak.

"Back off, Goody Two-Shoes, or you'll be next," snapped Stevely, without breaking her stride.

Then suddenly, 'WHOOSH!' a pair of Bunsen burners on either side of Stevely sprang into life, shooting fierce, foot-high flames into the air.

Everyone gasped. Kate stood her ground.

Stevely went pale and her hand trembled, almost spilling the contents of the test-tube down her own clothes... She hesitated, then took another step forward. She didn't want to lose face, despite her confusion.

As soon as she moved past them, the two Bunsen burners snuffed themselves out, as suddenly as they had ignited. It was as though her footfall had activated them. Her mouth went dry.

"I know what you're doing," she said to Kate. "You don't scare me!"

But Kate simply stood there, thin and tall in her ill-fitting uniform. She stared down at the advancing Stevely, a piercing look in her grey eyes.

Mel held her breath as Stevely approached the next pair of Bunsen burners and sure enough, a moment later, they too shot forth flames as if

Stevely had stepped across an invisible force field.

This time Mel was close enough to feel the intense heat herself. These flames were nothing like the weedy blue ones that Bunsen burners usually gave out. They were more like beacons, or distress flares.

What was happening? How could these burners suddenly come to life? Who was controlling them? *What* was controlling them?

Once again, as Stevely steeled herself and walked between the pair of Bunsen burners, the flames vanished.

By this time, the rest of the class was aghast. Those at the back, who hadn't had a clear view the first time the Bunsen burners ignited, had jostled their way to the front, or were standing on stools and craning their necks. Now, their mutterings of disbelief died down and an expectant hush fell as Stevely closed in on Kate.

Kate's eyes remained fixed on Stevely. She seemed unaware of anyone else in the Chemistry Lab.

Stevely steeled herself to brave the final set of Bunsen burners and close in on her victim. Three more paces ought to do it.

She took a step forward... then another...

She tilted the test-tube and made as if to throw

the contents over Kate's clothes.

Just one step closer and...

'SHOOM!' The Bunsen burners went up like rockets, twice as tall and ten times as hot as the previous flames. The onlookers drew back in utter horror and amazement. Stevely nearly jumped out of her skin.

The test-tube fell to the floor and shattered, spattering her feet and legs with little black dots, but leaving Kate's school uniform crisp, white and unblemished.

When Miss Goodall walked back into the lab a moment later, the Bunsen burners looked exactly as they had been when she left – lifeless – but the broken test-tube and upturned stools caught her eye.

"I come back to find nothing put away and damage to school property," she thundered. "I hold you ALL responsible for this abuse of my trust. When everything is cleaned and tidied up, you will all stay behind and copy out the periodic table in silence, until I dismiss you."

Still stunned and confused by what had happened, Class 8C didn't protest. In fact, everyone seemed almost relieved to be back in the normal world of shouting teachers and unfair punishments. The lab was tidied and the periodic table copied out.

It wasn't until afterwards, at the bus stop, that the talk turned to the astounding events in the lesson. Everyone was buzzing with talk of Stevely's bravado and the scary torches of flame.

Stevely was sure that Kate had tampered with the Bunsen burners. "It was Kate. She did it. I don't know how, but it was her," she said bitterly. "That weirdo could have burned me alive! And just look at my shoes! My dad'll kill me."

Mel didn't like to point out that the damage to Stevely's shoes was nothing compared to what Stevely had planned for Kate's blouse. Instead she nodded sympathetically while Stevely ranted, but all the time she was listening with half an ear to a conversation going on behind her.

"I tell you, I was standing closer to Kate than anyone. She didn't move a muscle, so how could she have switched the Bunsen burners on and off?" Clare was saying.

"Who else could have done it?" argued Tony. "She was the closest."

"I don't know. It's weird," Clare paused, then said thoughtfully: "The same kind of weird as that freak storm of papers in the history lesson the other day... and the way they seemed to attack Stevely." Her voice trailed off.

Mel shivered. It was true. Strange things seemed

to happen around Stevely lately... and it was always when she was picking on the new girl. All Kate seemed to do was to stare with those frightening, grey eyes of hers.

"What's the matter with you?" demanded Stevely, sulkily.

"Oh nothing," replied Mel, with a bright but unconvincing smile. Nothing like this had ever happened to Stevely before. Perhaps she was up against a whole lot more than she bargained for.

5

Poor little rich girl

By the following week, the events in the science lab were already beginning to find their way into the folklore of Cecily Fane High. But there were almost as many different versions of the story as there were people talking about it. Not only that, Class 8C were about evenly divided on who was to blame.

"If Kate wasn't such an oddball, Stevely wouldn't have picked on her in the first place. She brought it on herself," said one. "She's strange. No wonder Stevely calls her the Weirdo. She gives me the creeps."

"She can't help the way she looks. She doesn't deserve to be bullied because of it," said another.

"Yeah, you know what Stevely's like. If it hadn't been Kate, it would have been someone else. She went too far this time."

"Oh I did, did I?" said Stevely, looming up from nowhere, the way bullies do.

"Yes, you did," said the girl, meeting Stevely's gaze boldly. Mel was astonished. This was one of the 'plodders', as Stevely called them. There are a few of them in every class – the quiet, sensible, hard-working ones, who keep themselves to themselves and sink into the background at the first sign of trouble.

For once, Stevely was on the defensive.

"Well, she's no angel herself – look at that business with the Bunsen burners – she could have scarred me for life… "

"She never touched them, you know she didn't," interrupted another plodder.

"Oh no, who did then? An invisible ghost? Or was it one of you lot?" sneered Stevely, advancing on the girl with a hint of menace in her voice.

"Yeah, either she did it herself, or someone did it for her," put in Tony.

"You wait and see," muttered Stevely darkly. "I'm going to make that stuck-up weirdo pay for what she did to me." For the first time, Mel noticed, Stevely didn't sound quite so sure of herself as usual.

She must be losing her grip if even the plodders were beginning to stand up to her. Stevely would have to put Kate firmly in her place once and for all before things got out of hand.

From then on, Stevely seemed to think about nothing but Kate. It got very boring. Stevely's gang would be discussing the latest TV soap, or video game and Stevely would come up and say:

"You'll never guess what the Weirdo is up to now," or "That Kate is reading Charles Dickens in the bike shed again! I mean, get a life!"

Secretly, one or two of them couldn't see what was wrong with Kate reading a book if she felt like it. Stevely had done her best to make sure she didn't have any friends to talk to, after all. But they stopped short of saying this aloud.

One rainy break-time, Class 8C were sitting around their form room, chatting about the end of term trip to the Groombridge Heath Outward Bound Centre, which was a tradition at Cecily Fane High.

"We're going to have a midnight feast!" said one of the plodders, daringly.

"Oh, big deal!" said Stevely, "We're going to light

a campfire and barbecue Miss Goodall!" Most of the class laughed appreciatively.

"My dad's been giving me rock-climbing lessons, so I'll be able to beat the lot of you to the top of Groombridge Crags," boasted Jason.

"While those of us with brains will be using the dry slope ski lifts!" put in Stevely. Even Jason had to smile.

"And what are you most looking forward to about the school trip, Kate dear?" asked Stevely acidly.

Kate was sitting in a chair – rather than on a desk like most of them – and reading a magazine. She looked up slowly. "I'm sorry?" she said, her eyes fixed on Stevely.

"Oh, don't worry, you will be!" said Stevely, "We were just talking about the outward bound trip. We can guarantee you a thrilling time."

"Actually, I can't come," said Kate.

"Oh can't you, *actually*," mimicked Stevely cruelly. "Why's that then? Would you miss your elocution lessons? Or do you practise your crazy stare at weekends?"

The whole class laughed, egging Stevely on. Outside, the rain lashed against the windows.

"Oh, I get it. A school trip to an outward bound centre isn't good enough for you," she sneered. "I suppose you're used to skiing in St. Moritz? Yes, I can see that Groombridge Heath would be a bit of a come-down."

"I can't come because my family can't afford it at the moment," said Kate, her face and tone expressionless.

This was music to Stevely's ears. "Oh, too bad Cinderella, you *shan't* go to the ball," smirked Stevely. Then she started to chant quietly. "Poor little rich girl, poor little rich girl." The others joined in.

"Poor little rich girl, poor little rich girl," Mel heard herself singing, aware deep down that what she was doing was wrong, but unable to stop herself.

She ran a finger round the back of her collar. She felt unbearably hot. And now that she'd noticed it, the classroom itself was suddenly stifling. No movement stirred the air. It was like the hottest of summer days. Yet outside the rain poured down and gusts of wind blew leaves around the playground.

Mel went on singing, as if in a trance, but as she did so, she felt a tightening in the back of her throat. Suddenly it was difficult to breathe. Then she realized why. A faint haze of chalk dust hung in the air. She could see the tiny particles dancing before her eyes. But where had it come from?

At the same time, Mel noticed the chanting becoming fainter, as one by one, the voices trailed off in mid-sentence. And then she caught sight of the blackboard and her voice, too, faltered and stopped. A message was appearing in the chalk dust. A message written in spidery capitals. A message written by an unseen hand.

Everyone except Kate and Stevely was gaping at it in disbelief.

LEA wrote the invisible finger. *LEAV* Slowly, tortuously the words formed – *LEAVE* – and all the time the classroom grew hotter and hotter, stuffier and stuffier, until the air around the blackboard seemed to shimmer and the atmosphere was heavy with menace.

LEAVE HER

"Poor little rich girl, poor little rich..." At last, Stevely's voice also tailed off as she realized that she was the only one still singing.

She looked towards the classroom door guiltily, imagining that the others must have stopped because a teacher had walked in. Then her eyes fell on the blackboard and her knees almost buckled with the shock. An *A* was appearing, then an *L*, followed by *O*, *N* and *E*. The message was complete:

LEAVE HER ALONE

Mel could see that Stevely wanted to believe it was another of 'Kate's tricks'. But no one could have set this up. Some strange force was at work here... something unnatural... something *supernatural*.

Kate sat in silence at her desk, her eyes staring straight ahead and her body perfectly still. She was the only one who seemed unconcerned by what was going on around them. It was almost as if she wasn't really there.

Though she wouldn't admit it, Stevely was obviously afraid... very afraid.

6

Home truths?

Days passed and Mel had never seen Stevely so low. After the ghostly writing had appeared on the blackboard, it was as though all the stuffing had been knocked out of her. She was pale and distracted.

Occasionally, there would be flashes of the old Stevely – a cutting remark here and an outrageous boast there. But the strange events were already taking their toll.

There were jokes going around Cecily Fane High about 8C and all the spooky goings-on.

"Bet you don't know who's coming to visit 8C

next week?"

"Who?"

"The School In*spectre*, geddit?"

"Guess what! Because of 8C, the school's being renamed."

"Oh yes?"

"Yes. They're calling it the Cecily Fane High *Ghoul*!"

But to those who had witnessed the eerie goings-on, it was no laughing matter.

There was an uneasiness among everyone in the class... an uncomfortable feeling that somehow centred on the new girl with the strange, piercing stare.

Mel had mixed feelings about Stevely's withdrawn mood. She knew, deep down, that Stevely needed to be put in her place. After all, she *was* a bit of a bully. But Mel couldn't help missing her friend's breezy, happy-go-lucky attitude.

One afternoon in the playground, Mel even tried to renew Stevely's interest in teasing Kate – anything to cheer her up.

"I saw La Weirdo reading a French book in the bike shed again today," Mel joked.

"The witch, you mean," said Stevely quietly. "It was probably a book of spells."

"What?" asked Mel, surprised by the seriousness

in Stevely's voice.

"You heard me," said Stevely, with a sombre look on her face. "Kate the *witch*. That explains everything doesn't it? The papers, the Bunsen burners, the writing on the blackboard. We have a witch among us."

"You really think she *could* be a witch?" Mel asked nervously. She'd be a liar if she said that she hadn't been wondering the same thing.

"She could be," replied Stevely. "Witches don't have to be warty-nosed crones on broomsticks do they? Real ones, I mean."

"I suppose not," said Mel cautiously, uncertain what Stevely was really thinking.

"We need to know more," said Stevely. "We need to know what modern-day witches are supposed to be like. What they do, funny habits, that sort of thing. There was something about witches on TV last week, but my dad won't let me watch anything like that." Stevely was frowning.

From what Mel had gathered over the years, Stevely was a bit frightened of her dad. She never mentioned her mum at all.

"Yeah, I saw a bit of that programme," said Mel. "There were these women in Italy or somewhere, who held strange ceremonies in the woods. They formed a coven of white witches – you know what a coven is don't you, it's a group of..."

"I know what a coven is," snapped Stevely. "But this isn't Italy. We'll need more information than that to expose the Weirdo for what she is. I need you to go to the library for me, Mel."

"When?" asked Mel awkwardly, glancing down at her watch.

"After school today," said Stevely.

"Can't you go?" protested Mel.

"I've got to do something for my dad," Stevely explained.

"But I'm supposed to be going for a burger with my sister," Mel complained. Deep down, she knew that she'd end up having to do what Stevely wanted. "Anyway, what do you want from the library?"

"Think about it," said Stevely. "Everyone knows that there must be some link between Kate and the spooky things that have been happening in class lately..."

Stevely grinned for the first time in ages. "If you read up on modern-day witchcraft and we do a bit of careful planning, it ought to be easy enough to convince the rest of the class that Kate really is a witch!"

"So you want me to find out everything I can about witches?" asked Mel. She wondered how

Kate would react when she discovered Stevely's latest scheme.

"Exactly," nodded Stevely. "Even the plodders won't want to sit next to someone who might have a wax doll stuck full of pins in her locker!" she said with false cheerfulness.

What she didn't add was that Kate might just be downright dangerous.

"Okay," sighed Mel. "I'll go."

"Good," said Stevely. "I tell you what, I'll meet you afterwards, near the library. In *The Flying Pizza* at half past five. Then you can tell me what you've come up with."

"I don't even *like* pizza..." groaned Mel, but Stevely was already leaving.

So at five o'clock, when she should have been tucking into a *Megaburger* and fries, Mel found herself in Groombridge Public Library, browsing through a well-thumbed, weighty book called *Tobias Moon's Encyclopedia of the Paranormal*.

She flicked quickly through it from front to back, "Apparitions... Astral planes... Charms... Fortune-telling... Palmistry... Potions... Voodoo," at last, "Witches."

There were just a few paragraphs, but they didn't tell Mel anything that was likely to be much use to them.

WITCHES were women, accused of summoning up the power of the devil to aid them in their evil tasks. Throughout Western Europe in the 15th, 16th and 17th centuries, women accused of being witches were often persecuted and put to death.

The test to determine whether or not a woman was a witch was often a simple one – the ducking stool. The accused was tied to the stool and lowered beneath the water. If the woman drowned, she was obviously an ordinary human and was declared innocent (but dead). If she *didn't* drown she was deemed to be a genuine witch and was burned at the stake.

Witches were said to meet in groups of 13 called covens, to cast spells, to use charms, to turn into animals and to fly.

In the US, the most famous persecution against women accused of witchcraft was in Salem in 1692.

"It makes you think, doesn't it?" said a voice in her ear.

Mel almost jumped out of her skin. She spun around... There was nobody there. She looked down the row of shelves and thought that she glimpsed a flash of red hair disappearing behind a stack of books. Could it have been Kate? Perhaps she'd followed her.

"I said, it makes you think, doesn't it?" said the voice again.

Mel jolted her head back in surprise, and came face to face with a person holding a pile of books. She was a kindly-looking woman, thin and angular, with half-moon glasses perched on the end of her nose. She wore a badge marked 'LIBRARIAN'.

Why hadn't Mel seen her before? She must have been hidden by the corner of those shelves.

"I'm sorry. What?" asked Mel, trying to regain her composure.

The librarian pointed to the part of the encyclopedia that Mel had been studying. "The whole business about witches," she said. "I mean, you only had to be a single woman who didn't quite fit the mould and you became a social outcast at best. And at worst, you were drowned or burned... Thank goodness we live in more enlightened times!"

Social outcast... didn't quite fit the mould... If only she knew, thought Mel, suddenly realizing that she and Stevely were little better than witch-hunters themselves. Okay, they weren't actually planning to burn Kate but they *were* out to get her, just because she was different.

"I've got to go now," said Mel hurriedly. She almost knocked her chair over in her haste to return the book to the shelf.

As she lifted it up to put it back where it came from, it slipped from her grasp and fell to the floor with a resounding thud.

The book had fallen open at the "S" section and, just as Mel was bending down to pick it up, one of the definitions caught her eye:

A **SENSITIVE** is a person who is said to be a focus for psychic forces or spiritual interference from ghosts, poltergeists etc. A sensitive acts, wittingly or unwittingly, as an intermediary between the spiritual world of ghosts, ghouls and the restless dead, and the material world of our daily lives.

Spiritual interference can include: unexplained movement of inanimate objects; changes of temperature; surges of elemental energy (e.g. unexplained gusts of wind or spontaneous flames) and messages from beyond, which relate to the sensitive, or to those around them.

Many of the most widely documented cases of paranormal occurrences, and some of the most dangerous and horrifying, have been associated with people – usually girls – who are thought to be sensitives.

In 1979, the unexplained crash of a jumbo jet, following a freak fire, was blamed on the psychic forces of a famous sensitive, Maria Carlos. She was the only passenger on board to survive.

The gust of wind that blew the papers at Stevely... the Bunsen burners with lives of their own... the mysterious message on the blackboard. Suddenly it all made sense. Well, as much sense as anything so incredible *could* make.

This wasn't witchcraft they were faced with at Cecily Fane High. This was the work of *'ghosts, ghouls and the restless dead'* channelling their supernatural powers through a 'sensitive'... through Kate, the strange girl with the slate grey eyes.

Her pulse racing, Mel hurried to the photocopier with the encyclopedia. Her hands trembled as she placed the open book on top of the machine and fumbled to put a coin in the slot.

Stevely would never believe it unless she saw the description in black and white... Kate wasn't a witch. *She was haunted*!

7

34 Wisteria Gardens

Mel hurried into *The Flying Pizza*. She was five minutes late and Stevely was looking cross. "Where've you been?" she snapped.

"I had to use the photocopier," Mel replied. Stevely's irritation was of little importance after what she'd discovered.

"So it wasn't a wasted journey, then?" said Stevely, leaning forward eagerly, "What have you got for me? A recipe for boiled bat's blood?"

"No. This is serious, Stevely. I think maybe you should leave Kate alone from now on," said Mel. "She could be dangerous."

"What's got into you?" snorted Stevely. "I don't really believe the Weirdo's a witch, you know. I was only joking. I just wanted to see what you could come up with so that we can make the others believe it."

Mel unfolded the photocopy of the encyclopedia entry about sensitives and put it on the table in front of Stevely. "I don't think Kate's a witch either," Mel said quietly. "But I think I've found out what she really is." Mel watched carefully as Stevely read it through.

Good, she believes it too, thought Mel, as the look of triumph drained away from Stevely's face and was replaced first by a glimmer of recognition and then a look of fear. Like her, Stevely had obviously recognized the similarities between the events they'd witnessed in the classroom, and those connected to sensitives.

When Stevely reached the end of the entry, however, she tossed the photocopy aside. "Am I supposed to be impressed by this twaddle?" she said defiantly.

Far from warning Stevely off, as Mel hoped it would, the 'sensitive' theory seemed to have had the opposite effect. Mel should have known better.

The Flying Pizza was on the tatty side of Groombridge, a bus ride away from the smart new estate where Mel and Stevely lived. But the girls had just missed the 41 bus, so they decided to start walking.

"Look at the street names," said Mel, finding an excuse to steer the conversation away from Kate Thackery with her strange staring eyes and odd powers. She read off the names as they passed a series of side roads. "Lavender Crescent, Rose Hip Close – they sound really pretty. It's a shame they've ended up like this." She looked at the rows of once impressive houses decaying through neglect.

"Oh, I don't know," said Stevely, "All they need is a change of name to Crumbling Crescent, Rubbish Tip Close..." As they passed the next street, Stevely suddenly stopped and furrowed her brow. "Wisteria Gardens – that name rings a bell," she said.

Mel shrugged her shoulders.

"I've got it. This is where the Weirdo lives. It's Kate's street," said Stevely. "I remember she told one of the plodders that she'd moved to Wisteria Gardens. Number 34, I think. What a dump!"

"It looks creepy to me," muttered Mel. "Let's get a move on. The next bus is due in a minute."

But Stevely detected Mel's eagerness to get away and played on it. "Oh no, it's not every day you get to look at a witch's house. Let's go and listen out for some spells!" With a blood-curdling, horror-movie laugh, Stevely marched Mel down the street towards Number 34.

The houses in Wisteria Gardens must once have been the pride of Groombridge – they were even grander than those in the surrounding streets.

Number 34 was set apart slightly from the rest. It was at the farthest end from the main road, next to a scruffy clump of trees which some of the residents of Wisteria Gardens had used as a rubbish dump. When the girls approached the house, daylight had faded and the wind was stirring the branches of the trees, making them creak and groan ominously.

Two gnarled old yew trees stood at either side of the front gate like sentinels, and although they cast a threatening shadow over Mel and Stevely, the girls were glad of the camouflage.

"We don't want Kate's batty old aunt inviting us in for an arsenic sandwich!" said Stevely. Her voice trembled slightly, despite her attempts at humour. "She probably taught Kate everything she knows!"

The house towered above them. Weathered gargoyles grimaced down from turrets. A shutter banged against a wrought iron balcony. Arched, leaded windows gave the house a church-like air and the dead looking branches of a gnarled creeper climbed everywhere, over windows, drainpipes and doors.

"Well, I've seen enough," said Mel. "Let's go home now. This place is giving me the creeps." She didn't say so, but she'd also remembered the encyclopedia, the bit about the sensitive who'd caused a plane crash. She really didn't want to come face to face with Kate on her home ground.

But, whether it was to tease her friend or just because she was intrigued by the spooky old pile, Stevely wouldn't budge.

"No, wait," she insisted. "If only we could get close enough to look through the windows. We might be able to spot something that we could use to persuade the others that she really is a witch – a black cat or something."

But Mel was in no mood to make fun of Kate now. "Let's go," she repeated.

"No way," said Stevely firmly but, as she pushed open the rusty old gate, her hand trembled slightly. Mel noticed and realized that her friend wasn't quite as tough as she seemed.

Wincing as the gate creaked, the two girls slipped through it as quietly as they could and sank quickly back into the shadows of the shrubbery.

They crept through the undergrowth, their hearts racing and their breathing shallow. Soon, they reached a gap in the bushes, from where they could see some french windows at the side of the house.

"Come on! It's all quiet. Let's go for it!" whispered Stevely. Mel hesitated. Those last three yards would take them out of the cover of the shrubbery and into full view of anyone on their side of the house...

Nothing stirred. Mel braced herself.

Just as they were about to set off, a sudden movement from an upper window made them freeze in their tracks. A pair of curtains was thrown back to reveal a square of yellow light... and the black silhouette of Kate herself.

Despite the distance and the fact that she and Stevely were hidden in the shrubs and shadows, Mel somehow *knew* that Kate could see them. She felt Kate's staring eyes upon her, sensed the same reproachful glare that had so unnerved her that very first day in the school canteen.

Mel ran, with Stevely close behind.

8

The girl in the picture

"Witchypoos!" hissed Stevely as Kate walked into the Art room the next morning. A few people tittered, but others gave Stevely withering glances. She was losing her grip.

Kate just ignored her. She picked her way through the desks and easels to take up the only vacant seat which was at the back of the room, in between Mel and Clare.

Today, Mr. Sanderson, their art teacher, was feeling inspired. "Now then 8C," he said, nervously twiddling the end of his droopy moustache. "I want us to try something a bit different, this lesson. I want you to do a drawing or painting – I don't mind what the subject is – that really says something about *you*, the person..."

There were a number of groans, but Mr. Sanderson appeared not to hear them.

"It must be a subject you really care about. It might be an abstract sketch expressing a strong feeling – perhaps working with the textures of charcoal on rough paper," he continued. "Or it could be a watercolour of a person, or an object, or a place that has some true significance to you, the artist. Is that clear?"

There was an unenthusiastic murmur of "Yes, Mr. Sanderson."

"Good," said the teacher. "When I look at your pictures, I want to be able to experience that true feeling... I want to be able to learn more about you, just by studying your work. Okay? Get started."

Mel's heart sank. At the moment the only thing she felt passionate about was the bell ringing to end the lesson, but she couldn't draw that.

Already some of her classmates were making a start. Tony had begun a painstaking drawing of the emblem of his favourite football team. Clare had taken a pink-haired troll out of her pencil case and was trying to capture its leering grin on paper. Stevely – she might have known – was squinting into a make-up mirror, attempting a self-portrait.

Mel stared into space, desperately searching for some inspiration. She saw Kate leaning intently over her easel already hard at work. Her head was cocked to one side as if she was listening to an inward voice. Her hand flew across the paper making bold, confident strokes, first with a piece of charcoal, then a paintbrush. And all the time, her body trembled with concentration, right to the ends of her frizzy red hair.

Kate must feel pretty strongly about something, to go at it like *that*, Mel thought, though she couldn't actually see the painting... Had Kate really been able to see them from the window the previous night? Or had Mel's mind been playing tricks? Things seemed less certain in the cool light of day...

As the lesson wore on, Mr. Sanderson started doing the rounds, giving advice. Mel began scribbling desperately, trying to get something down on paper before he got round to her.

"Is that a self-portrait, Stevely?" asked the art teacher, approaching the back row.

"Or a poster for King Kong?" someone quipped in a stage whisper.

Stevely pouted, "It's this mirror, Mr. Sanderson, it just isn't big enough!"

"No," sniggered Matt, "but could there *be* one big enough for your head, Stevely?"

The whole class fell about. It made a change for Stevely to be the butt of the jokes. Strange really, Mel wouldn't have believed it a few weeks ago.

Mr. Sanderson had worked his way round to Kate. He stood behind her in silence for a moment or two.

"Remarkable!" he said. "Have you really done all this today?" Kate nodded. "Well you obviously have a gift for figure work. Do you mind if I show it to the class?"

"No," murmured Kate. She hardly seemed aware of her classmates at all. She had the distant, distracted air of someone in a trance.

"Who is the girl in the picture?" the teacher asked. "Your sister? A friend?"

"Martha," said Kate, barely louder than a whisper. "Her name was... her name is Martha."

As Mr. Sanderson held the painting up to a stunned 8C, Stevely stood behind him poking one finger into her open mouth, as if to make herself sick. No one laughed.

In the time it had taken Mel to do a rough pencil sketch of her trainer and then rub half of it out again, Kate had sketched, then painted, something remarkable. Her picture showed a frail girl – Kate had called her Martha – in old-fashioned clothes, standing on a windswept moorland at night.

Mr. Sanderson went into raptures over it. "See the pathos in Martha's hand, as it clutches her thin shawl around her shoulders – doesn't it make you feel sorry for her?

"Look at the way the moonlight accentuates her pale face, giving her a haunting quality and making her seem almost transparent. And her eyes... Well, if I could paint raw emotion as Kate has captured it in those eyes, I wouldn't need to *teach* art, I can tell you!"

Usually this kind of praise from a teacher would have the whole class heaving, and the unlucky pupil would be writhing in his or her seat with embarrassment. But everyone, even Stevely, now that she'd caught sight of the picture, seemed mesmerized.

It was a strangely unsettling portrait. The background was so realistic that you felt as though you, too, were being buffeted by the storm, Mel thought. Yet the girl in the picture seemed somehow distant.

Something about the way Kate had painted Martha, gave her a ghostly quality – as though, if you took your eyes off her, she might disappear. But her expression of suffering was so real and sincere that to look away felt like a betrayal.

When the bell rang for break, Stevely started helping Mr. Sanderson tidy away the art materials. Mel knew something was afoot.

"Thank you, Stevely," said a grateful and rather surprised Mr. Sanderson. "If you could just put that folder of work carefully in the stockroom, please. It's all to go on display at tomorrow's parents' evening. I'm off to the Staff Room for a well-deserved cuppa. Don't forget to lock up."

"Of course, Mr. Sanderson," said Stevely, as though butter wouldn't melt in her mouth.

Mel noticed Stevely smirk behind her hand. Something told her that they hadn't heard the last of Kate's painting.

9

An invitation

Mel's sense of foreboding turned out to be justified. The next morning when Mrs. Bannister was taking the register, Mr. Sanderson came marching into 8C's classroom fizzing with rage.

He unfurled a large piece of paper that he'd been carrying under his arm and held it up, wordlessly, before the class. A gasp of horror went up.

Kate's powerful portrait of Martha on the moor – Mr. Sanderson's prize exhibit for parents' evening – was ruined. Someone had added a beard, moustache and glasses, all scribbled hastily in thick black felt pen.

Mel shot a worried glance at Kate, whose face was drained of colour. Yet she didn't look angry. In fact, Mel thought she looked sad and a little afraid.

It appeared that Stevely was Mr. Sanderson's number one suspect. "Are you sure you know nothing about this?" he demanded sternly, fixing her with a penetrating glare. "You were the last one in the Art Room yesterday – the *only* one who had the opportunity."

"No, Mr. Sanderson," said Stevely, opening her eyes very wide and shaking her head earnestly. "Someone must have sneaked in after I'd finished clearing up. I'm afraid I must have forgotten to lock the door."

"And no one else will own up?" demanded Mr. Sanderson. "None of the other classes knew about Kate's picture, so it has to be one of you." There was silence. "Fine," he fumed. "Then all of you except Kate will have detention."

There were murmurs of discontent among Stevely's classmates.

"She really *has* gone too far this time," Clare whispered to Jason.

Mutinous talk like this among Stevely's gang would have been unthinkable a few weeks ago. Now Mel found herself silently agreeing with them.

After the act of vandalism was discovered, Stevely became very jumpy. She had acted in haste when she ruined Kate's painting and now she was beginning to regret it. Every time someone slammed a classroom door or dropped a book, she flinched and shot a nervous glance at Kate.

She's waiting for some supernatural revenge, thought Mel. Deep down she knows as well as I do that it's dangerous to tangle with Kate. All those weird things – the flying papers, the Bunsen burners and the letters on the blackboard – they all happened after Stevely had taunted Kate.

But Stevely just can't help it, thought Mel. Stevely *has* to be Number One.

As for the expected attack, nothing happened. Kate was perfectly civil to Stevely, and continued to be friendly and natural with anyone who treated her the same way.

Even Matt had begun to talk to Kate again, and didn't seem to care too much what Stevely thought about it any more.

On Wednesday, Kate walked into the playground and started handing out pieces of paper. "I wonder what she's up to?" said Mel.

"She's probably passed some superswots' French exam and is passing around copies of her certificate," tittered Stevely. "Or, perhaps she's painted another masterpiece or two."

They soon found out what it was. Mel wished she could have taken a snapshot of Stevely's face when Kate came up and handed each of them a slip of yellow paper, printed on a computer. It read:

```
    IT'S MY BIRTHDAY ON SATURDAY
 so come and help me celebrate with
          a pizza and a video
        at 34 Wisteria Gardens
          East Groombridge


               7 - 10pm
                RSVP
```

"I hope you can both make it," said Kate, smiling. "The others are coming." Mel waited anxiously to take her cue from Stevely.

At first her friend seemed too astonished to utter a word. But then she shot a knowing glance at Mel and said with heavy sarcasm "What, us? Miss the social event of the decade? Just try and keep us away!"

The truth was that Stevely was unsure what to do. Go to Kate's party? Somehow, that'd be like admitting defeat. But there was her gang to think about.

Stevely wasn't too happy about the way things were going. Clare, Jason and Matt were already chatting openly about the party on Saturday night. And none of them thought to ask whether she would be there. No, Stevely would go to 34 Wisteria Gardens all right, and she'd be in the centre of the action.

Saying goodbye at the end of school on Friday, Stevely grinned at Mel. "See you at Kate's party tomorrow night," she said. "I'll give her a birthday to remember!"

10

Party party!

When Mel and Stevely arrived outside 34 Wisteria Gardens on Saturday evening, the atmosphere couldn't have been more different from the eerie quiet that had shrouded it the previous week.

Fairy lights were strung across the verandah and a hand-painted banner read 'HAPPY BIRTHDAY KATE'. Music wafted out of an open window, along with snatches of chatter and peals of laughter.

"Hi, come in," smiled Kate, opening the front door. "I'm just opening my presents and then we can order some pizzas."

"I'm afraid I haven't had time to get you anything, Kate," muttered Mel, sheepishly. She was quite taken aback when Stevely felt in her pocket and pulled out a small, beautifully wrapped package.

"Happy Birthday, Kate," Stevely smirked. Kate took the package gingerly, as if it might go off, but she remembered her manners.

"Thanks, Stevely. You didn't need to... "

"Me? Not get you a present? Why, Kate, the very idea," Stevely interrupted in a sugary voice, as though she was Kate's oldest and dearest friend.

Mel waited anxiously for Kate to tear off the patterned paper. She knew there had to be a catch, but at first glance Stevely's present looked innocent enough. It was wrapped in cellophane and stapled to a gaudy piece of card. But when Kate turned it over and read the printing on the package, her face fell. 'Witches' Warts' it said.

Sure enough, through the cellophane could be seen half a dozen revolting plastic pimples that you were meant to lick and stick on your face.

"Fake warts for a fake witch!" hissed Stevely, "I hope you like them!" and with that, she swaggered into the drawing room, to ruin everyone else's evening.

"Take no notice," said Mel nervously putting a

sympathetic hand on Kate's shoulder, "It's just Stevely's way."

Kate smiled strangely. "Don't worry," she said, looking down at the fake warts. "They're very... very *appropriate*, considering my Aunt Cordelia's line of work." She turned suddenly and walked off down the hall.

Mel wondered what she could have meant by that? These days, just looking into Kate's slate grey eyes was enough to send her imagination into overdrive.

Now Mel was alone, she looked around the hall. It was an amazing room, just like a movie set. There was a stag's head over the front door, an elegant curving staircase with a carved banister and a suit of armour on the half-landing. Gloomy oil paintings in heavy gilt frames hung on every wall.

Kate reappeared. Perhaps she felt terrible being the butt of Stevely's nastiness but, if so, she was brilliant at hiding it.

"Let's join the others, shall we?" suggested Kate and they walked into the drawing room.

Stevely had already managed to pour cold water on the party atmosphere. In the short time since she had arrived, she had ridiculed Kate's tape collection, compared the furnishings in the drawing room to a junk shop and was now reading aloud from the pizza menu and making supposedly witty asides:

"Listen to this one. *'The Bucking Bronco*. Hot and spicy ground beef topping that packs quite a punch.' Sounds like one for you Jason." Jason smiled wanly. "And here's one for Kate. *'Pizza Quattro Formaggi* – a delicate blend of four fine Italian cheeses. One for the connoisseur'. Sounds snooty enough for her, don't you think?"

When Stevely saw the two girls enter together, a frown of irritation crossed her face. "You'll have a difficult choice, Mel, you don't even *like* pizza, do you?" she added.

"Don't worry", replied Mel, looking daggers at Stevely and determined not to spoil Kate's birthday. "I didn't *used* to like pizza."

"That's lucky," said Kate, picking up the handset of an amazing old-fashioned telephone. "Let's order!"

11

Stevely lends a hand

"The pizzas will be here in half an hour," announced Kate, putting the phone down. "Anybody need a drink?"

"Yeah," said Stevely, looking down her nose at the cans of fizzy drink that her friends were enjoying. "Is that all you've got?"

Kate was unfazed. "Sorry, Stevely," she said. "All we have is cola, orange juice, lemonade or ginger beer."

"Are you sure you aren't hiding away some witches' brew for later on?" she sniggered. "Where have you hidden your cauldron, huh?"

She began 'searching' every nook and cranny in the room. It was obvious to everyone that the cauldron jibe was just Stevely's excuse for a good snoop. Watching her, they felt awkward and uneasy.

She rifled through cupboards and rearranged ornaments. She looked behind chairs and even in the coal scuttle.

Finally Stevely lifted the lid of an old roll-top desk and grabbed the first thing she could get hold of inside. She recoiled in horror.

It was a limp, white hand... a *severed* hand. Torn veins dangled from the hacked wrist, and globules of blood caught the light sickeningly. The others looked on in utter amazement.

Then Clare screamed.

In blind panic, Stevely threw the hideous thing away from her. The others watched, appalled, as it flew through the air, and landed in Matt's lap...

... It was only when the gang noticed the corners of Kate's mouth twitching, that Matt plucked up the courage to take a closer look.

"It's all right Stevely, it's not real!" he said, laughing. "But it had me worried for a minute."

Everyone let out a sigh as a wave of relief flooded the room. Jason passed the fake hand to Clare who fingered it gingerly and agreed that it had exactly the colour and texture of real flesh.

"Here, Stevely, have another look!" laughed Jason, holding the severed hand out politely to her, as if to shake hands.

Stevely sank back in her chair, holding her own cupped hand in front of her mouth and shook her head violently. Her face was pale green.

"Quite convincing, isn't it?" said Kate. "My Aunt Cordelia made it for a horror movie called 'The Hand of Doom'. It makes a great paperweight!"

Mel smiled. What was it Kate had said about the fake witches' warts Stevely had given her? 'They're very appropriate, considering my Aunt Cordelia's line of work.'

It turned out that Kate's Aunt Cordelia used to work in horror movies for one of the big film studios. She looked after the props department. When the studio went bust, she'd bought some of her favourite props at knockdown prices.

It all made sense now, thought Mel. No wonder the house had such a weird, unreal atmosphere. It was half genuine and half make-believe. She had thought the stag's head and suit of armour in the hall were a bit over the top. Now Kate explained that they had come from the set of a whodunnit called 'Murder Most Lethal'.

"Hey, Kate," said Matt, now fully recovered from the practical joke. "Are all the rooms like this? Can we have a look round?"

"Of course," said Kate. "Are you coming Stevely?" Stevely shook her head. She was still nursing her hurt pride. She could have kicked herself for acting like a fool over that stupid hand.

Kate's no sensitive, thought Stevely. The flying papers, Bunsen burners and spooky writing were probably nothing more than elaborate hoaxes staged with the help of her batty old aunt.

As her friends' footsteps grew fainter and their excited chatter died away, Stevely sat for a moment or two, staring moodily round the vast drawing room, wondering which were the real antiques and which were the film props.

The carved wooden candelabra hanging from the ceiling, with its miniature gargoyles, flying bats and dripping candle wax, must surely have been made for some third-rate horror film.

Even so, Stevely admitted to herself, the overall effect of the room was pretty atmospheric... Suddenly, the french windows behind her flew open with a crash, and the muslin curtains billowed into the room. Stevely felt a chill on the back of her neck.

She got up and whirled round, but there was no

one to be seen. Was this just a faulty window catch on a windy night, or something more? Stevely didn't stick around to find out.

"Wait for me, you lot!" she called, dashing out of the room and taking the stairs two at a time. She lurched round the half-landing and almost cannoned into the others.

"Changed your mind, Stevely?" asked Jason, with an amused grin. "Or did you get lonely?"

"I'm looking for the toilet if it's any of your business," she lied, as casually as her pounding heart and panting breath would let her.

Stevely was losing her grip. No one seemed afraid of her any more. Tonight she would have to sort out Kate Thackery once and for all.

12

Secrets

"So where's your Aunt Cordelia now, Kate?" asked Clare. They were exploring the winding staircases and labyrinthine passages of the old house.

"Oh, she went out with mum and dad to visit some friends. They won't be back for ages," Kate replied.

Kate's bedroom was amazing, though Mel wasn't sure that she'd get much sleep if it was hers. It was a little too macabre for that.

The room was reached by a spiral staircase and was hexagonal. The arched, leaded windows gave the place a fairytale atmosphere and a wrought iron bed with a canopy drew gasps of admiration.

A collection of stuffed birds and animals in glass cases stared out into the room with beady, knowing eyes.

"Don't they give you the creeps?" Matt asked Kate, meeting the unblinking gaze of a tawny owl.

"No. I think of them as friends," Kate replied.

"Sad!" whispered Stevely to Mel, passing an old dressing table with a broken mirror. "Look into it once too often, did you?" she asked Kate.

Throughout the house, dusty, velvet drapes bordered with moth-eaten gold tassels added to the air of mystery, and grimy old oil paintings of Kate's long-dead ancestors seemed to lurk round every corner. Mel was sure she saw the eyes move on one of them, as she started to walk away. She shivered.

There was even a lethal-looking guillotine which turned out to have a fibreglass blade. In another corner, a life-size ventriloquist's dummy grinned at them from a rocking chair.

"Gottle o' Geer," said Tony, shaking the dummy by its stiff, wooden hand. He leaped back in surprise.

"It's alive!" he shouted, then added: "Fooled you!" as the gang scrambled for the door.

Giggling, but still deliciously spooked, they jostled their way down a passageway.

Finding himself at the back of the line as they traipsed off to look at the guest room, Tony noticed a narrow corridor which he'd missed before. At the far end, all alone, was a little door. He crept down the passage to have a look.

It didn't seem as though anyone had been this way for a long time. Cobwebs trembled as he slunk past them, and every so often a floorboard gave a tell-tale creak.

He glanced nervously behind him, not sure whether he was checking to see if one of the gang had spotted him, or whether some more sinister character was on his tail.

At last Tony came to a door. He felt his heart hammering in his chest. His palms were moist and he held his breath as he twisted the door handle this way and that.

It was almost a relief when the door wouldn't open. He turned around and started walking back, a little faster than was really necessary, down the corridor. But before he was halfway along it, he heard the squeak of rusty hinges coming from behind him. The locked door wasn't locked any more...

Tony glanced over his shoulder and saw a dark

shape emerge from the doorway. He couldn't see very well, but the half-light was good enough to tell that it wasn't... *human*. Then came a rumbling sound. Whatever it was, it was moving towards him and gathering speed.

Tony started to run, but the thing was gaining on him. He heard the 'thrum' of wheels hitting uneven floorboards and he shot a second, terrified glance over his shoulder.

What he saw made him catch his breath. An old-fashioned pram was thundering towards him... but that was no *baby* inside it. The pram was carrying an adult dressed in a mob cap and shawl – an adult skeleton, its face leering at him with a rictus of death.

13

The skeleton in the closet

Tony opened his mouth to scream, but no sound came. All he could manage was a whimpering cry of "H-e-e-e-l-p!" before diving into a nearby alcove.

He covered his eyes, but felt the bony fingers of the skeleton rake his hair as the pram whizzed past him.

There was an almighty 'THUD' and then, a few seconds later, a sickening clatter. Peering out between his fingers, Tony saw the empty pram lying on its side on the landing. There was no sign of its unfortunate passenger.

The friends came rushing back from the guest room to find out what had happened.

"Tony, are you all right?"

"What happened, Tony?"

"Tony, speak to me!"

Tony lay on the floor gesturing towards the pram and gabbling senselessly.

Kate saw the open door at the end of the passage and the empty pram on the landing. She peered over the stair rail and caught her breath. Far below her, scattered across the tiled floor of the hall, lay a heap of broken bones, a shawl and a mob cap. She put two and two together, and started to chuckle.

As far as Mel could remember, this was the first time she had ever heard Kate laugh. Then again, this was the first time she'd been with Kate outside school, and Kate didn't have much to laugh *about* at Cecily Fane High.

It was a strange laugh – slightly nervous and probably unfamiliar even to Kate herself.

"Oh, Tony. Poor you," she said. "That was Esmerelda."

"It... It came at me... Out of that room ... It was... t-t-terrifying," stammered Tony.

Seeing how genuinely frightened Tony was, Kate's expression turned to one of concern. "There's nothing to worry about, Tony. Honestly," she said, hurriedly explaining that the room was 'Aunt Cordelia's overflow' – a store room crammed to the ceiling with all the theatrical bric a brac that Aunt Cordelia hadn't found a place for in the rest of the house.

"We used to keep Esmerelda out on the verandah, but the paperboy wouldn't set foot in the drive, so Aunt Cordelia put her in here, out of harm's way."

"B-but, if she's only a prop, how did she get out? I tried the door and it was locked," said Tony, still recovering from the shock.

"It doesn't actually lock, but it sometimes sticks. When you tried the handle, you must have loosened the mechanism," Kate explained. "Then, when you started to walk away, it sprang open by itself."

"The floorboards seem to slope down towards this end of the corridor," Jason pointed out. "Once the pram was moving, it would have kept on gathering speed."

Tony smiled wanly, "Thanks for the explanation, professor."

Everyone laughed and started to make their way down the back stairs. The route took them past the only room in the house, besides the kitchen, which they hadn't yet explored. But Kate seemed in a hurry to usher them past it.

"Hey, what about this room, Kate?" asked Matt, "Don't we get to look in here?"

Kate stiffened. "No," she said firmly. "No one is allowed in there." Her voice was rising. "*No one.* Not even me. *Is that clear*?"

There was an uncomfortable silence.

"I suppose that's the Rooom of Dooom that's filled with Glooom?" Jason grinned, trying to lighten the atmosphere.

Some of the others laughed, but Mel wasn't one of them. Her eyes were on Kate. Whatever was in that room was no laughing matter to Kate.

A moment later, the doorbell rang. The forbidden room was soon forgotten, as they charged down the hall shouting: "Pizza! Yeaaaaaah!"

Forgotten, that is, by everyone but Stevely, who had been standing silently in the shadows. She paused for a moment outside the heavy oak door, with its small oval plaque, bearing just one word:

NURSERY

As Stevely stood there, on the threshold of the unknown, she could feel her palms getting clammy. Her heartbeat raced and her nerves jangled. No way was Kate going to tell *her* what to do. No way could Kate stop her entering this room. Stevely had made up her mind. Before the evening was over, she was going to discover the secrets of the nursery.

14

Lights out!

Jason was first to the front door. He threw it open eagerly. "Sorry you've had a long wait," said what appeared to be a stack of pizza boxes on legs.

"Uhuh?" replied Jason, baffled, for a moment, by this strange sight.

"The weather's taken a turn for the worst. I'm getting behind with all my deliveries," explained the pizza delivery man, peering round the side of the boxes with an apologetic grin. Jason stepped outside and looked up at the big clouds gathering in the moonlit sky.

"Mmmm. Looks as though we're in for a storm,"

Jason said to Kate as she paid the pizza man.

"Never mind, it'll be nice and cosy inside," said Kate, her eyes glinting in the moonlight. She led the way back to the drawing room to share out the food and open more cans of drinks.

There was some good-natured squabbling about who ordered which pizza but, before long, they were munching away greedily.

"Now it's time to watch the horror video," Kate announced, switching on the video player.

"What have you got for us, Kate, one of your home movies?" Jason asked good-naturedly. "I can't think of anything spookier than this place!"

"No, not quite," Kate grinned.

Stevely rolled her eyes. "Is it in French?" she mocked. "I'm sure *all* your favourite films are in French."

"Shhhh!"

"Shut up, Stevely, we'll miss the start," said Tony crossly.

And at that moment, the title of the video came up on the screen in huge letters, dripping blood:

"Great!" said Clare, snuggling into a corner of a battered sofa, with a slice of pizza, a can of lemonade and a cushion.

"Excellent choice, Kate," whispered Tony. Stevely scowled at him.

"Yeah. I bet no one else at school has seen this," added Jason.

Even Stevely couldn't help feeling a pleasurable thrill of excitement as the opening sequence began. There was an aerial shot of a decaying graveyard, with eerie organ music in the background...

Suddenly a blinding flash turned the windows into sheets of brilliant light. It was followed by an almighty blast, then the room was plunged into darkness.

Someone screamed.

Chaos broke out. Cans of drink were kicked over and pizza was mangled underfoot.

Then there was another flash followed by a deep, rumbling boom of thunder that felt as though it came from the very bowels of the house.

"The lightning must have brought down a power cable," said Kate's voice. "Don't worry. I'll light some candles."

Slowly the features of the room re-emerged from the pitch dark in shadowy form, as Kate lit candles and positioned them around the room. When she could see what she was doing, she stood on a chair and lit the gruesome candelabra that Stevely had noticed earlier.

Illuminated, it was even more effective. Each candle was carefully positioned to throw the huge shadow of a gargoyle or a bat onto the walls and ceiling. As the candles burned down, the shadows would change shape and position, making the room seem inhabited by demons.

Mel stood up and admired the effect. "You should have thought of this before," she said. "It creates just the right atmosphere for a horror movie."

"Well, it's too late now," scoffed Stevely. "The only horror picture Kate'll be seeing tonight is her sensitive little face in that broken mirror in her bedroom!"

Sensitive? Mel wondered if Stevely had deliberately chosen that word. She shuddered at the sudden recollection of Kate's other side. Despite the spooky surroundings, Kate had seemed so human this evening... but who knew what supernatural forces might be at work in the house of a 'sensitive'?

"Take no notice of Stevely, Kate," said Matt, ignoring Stevely's angry glance. "Why don't we all tell each other ghost stories?"

Matt took one of the fat yellow candles from the mantelpiece and placed it on a little table in the middle of the room. They all sat in a circle around it, their features completely transformed. Suddenly, they weren't a group of friends from Class 8C any more, but eerie strangers, their faces wreathed in light and shade.

"Right!" said Matt. "Who's going to tell the first ghost story?"

"What about you, Kate?" Mel asked, the words from the encyclopedia of the paranormal fixed clearly in her mind: *'A sensitive acts... as an intermediary between the spiritual world of ghosts, ghouls and the restless dead, and the material world of our daily lives.'* "I'm sure you must know some ghost stories."

"Yeah," said Jason. "Mr. Sanderson did say that your painting of that girl had a *haunting* quality."

"It was spooky," Clare nodded in the flickering light. "What did you say the girl's name was?"

"Martha," said Kate, looking deep into Clare's eyes. "Her name is Martha." She scanned each of their strangely-lit faces, as if trying to decide whether she could trust them. "And, yes, I know a story about her, only it's not an ordinary ghost story because it's true. And I'm a part of it too. It's the story of what happened in this house... and of the strange events at school."

No one noticed Stevely slip out of the room. It was dark and, anyway, she was doing her best not to be seen. Stevely didn't want to hang around while Kate took centre stage. Besides, she had something far more important to do. She wanted to investigate the nursery.

It was almost as if something was pulling her to the room like metal to a magnet. She couldn't get it out of her mind. She had to see what lay the other side of the nursery door. Gingerly, she stepped into the hallway.

15

Kate's story

"I suppose, for you lot, the story began when I first joined your class and weird things started to happen whenever I got really upset," Kate began. "For me, it started before that, one day when I went for a walk in the churchyard. For Martha, it must have started over a hundred years ago in this very house." Kate stared into the candle flame.

"But this is my story, so I'll start with my trip to the churchyard, not long after we moved here. My great-great grandfather was brought up in this house. My aunt told me he'd had several brothers and sisters who'd also lived here, but they died

81

when they were young. I didn't really think anything of it until I saw the name 'Thackery' in the churchyard.

"I came across some old gravestones that were smaller than usual. The writing on them was very worn, but I could just about make out enough letters to know that the surnames were 'Thackery', like mine.

"It was a shock when I read the words, 'went to sleep, age 6' on one of them. It's horrible to think about anyone dying so young. But these children were my great-great aunts and uncles, yet I'm already older than they ever lived to be.

"As I was standing there in the churchyard, the sun went in and a shadow fell across one of the headstones. I heard a voice carried towards me on the breeze. It was a child's voice, crying faintly. *'Kate, Kate, help us!'*

"I was really spooked by it. I couldn't see anyone, but I knew I wasn't imagining it. The voice seemed to come from nowhere. *'Help us!'* it cried again and again. I wanted to run, but the voice was still speaking. What it said next made no sense, but I can remember the words exactly. *'Reveal her for what she was. Avenge the wrongs of the past. Set our souls to rest!'*

"'Who's there?' I called out. I knew I was playing

with fire, but whoever it was sounded so sad.

"Then the voice grew louder and more desperate still. I panicked. The words *'Help us! Help u-u-us!'* were ringing in my ears, as I ran out of the church yard. I didn't stop till I got home!

"I tried not to think about what had happened. I tried to tell myself that my mind was playing tricks on me. Then, the day before I started school – I remember because I'd washed my hair specially – I was combing it through at the dressing table. You know, the one in my room with the broken mirror, only it wasn't broken then.

"One minute, everything was normal, and the next the mirror misted over right in front of me. Letters started to appear on the glass... it looked just as if someone had breathed on it and was writing with an invisible finger."

Mel gasped inaudibly and glanced at the others. The look on their faces said it all. Recognition tinged with fear. They were remembering the chilling message that had appeared in the chalk dust on the blackboard at school.

Kate continued to stare into the flickering flame of the candle on the table. "The message on the mirror read 'Cecily Fane'."

"Our school?" said Tony, looking puzzled. "Are you trying to tell me that a ghost – or whatever –

wrote the name of our school on your mirror?"

Clare shook her head, baffled. Matt gave Kate a suspicious glance. Was she teasing them? As far as they knew, Cecily Fane was some boring old Victorian do-gooder, who'd had more money than sense. Unfortunately for them, she'd decided to spend some of it founding a school – their school. What could this have to do with Kate's long-dead relations?

There was a tremor in Kate's voice as she continued. "I said aloud, 'What do you want? Are *you* Cecily Fane?' but, before I'd even had a chance to finish the question, the mirror shattered, all by itself. It was as if it'd been punched in anger by an invisible fist.

"It's hard to describe, but I could somehow feel *rage* everywhere around me. Whoever was trying to communicate with me obviously *hated* Cecily Fane. But why? I mean, what did it have to do with me?

"Later that night I found out. I was lying in bed, trying to get to sleep, but I knew it was no good. I felt restless, thinking back to the voice in the graveyard and the writing on the mirror. I kept tossing and turning, and all the time the words 'Cecily Fane' crept into my thoughts and the child's voice kept crying: *'Help us! Reveal her for what she* was. *Avenge the wrongs of the past. Set our souls to rest!'*

"Then I realized the child's voice wasn't in my head. It was... it was in the room with me. I wasn't alone any more... and I haven't been alone since."

Mel dropped her empty can with a clatter. The others shuffled uneasily. No one took their eyes off Kate. There was an energy around her that almost crackled.

"The voice was saying my name, over and over again," Kate continued in a quiet monotone, as she seemed to relive the experience. "I sat up and there she was, standing at the end of my bed."

"*She?*" asked Tony. "Who?"

"Martha," said Kate. "The girl in my painting. I could see her with my own eyes, and I knew at once that it was *her* voice calling me in the churchyard, *her* finger writing the message on my mirror. And now she was in my room, as close to me as you are, and seeming just as real.

"If I'd wanted to, I could have reached out and touched her. But something stopped me. Maybe it was her old-fashioned clothes, maybe it was something else. I knew that if I put out my hand, it would have gone right through her..."

16

Martha's tale

As the gang took in the terrible meaning of Kate's words, another flash of lightning lit up the room with brilliant whiteness and a thunderbolt exploded like a bomb.

But still all eyes were on Kate. She paused to let the thunder subside, before continuing.

"The girl's cheeks were as pale as a corpse and there was a very unhappy look on her face," said Kate. "Her arms and legs were all skinny, and she clutched her shawl around her shoulders, as if she'd never feel warm again.

"'Who are you?' I demanded.

"It was then that she told me her name and began her grim tale. She only had a short life, but it was such an unhappy one."

Kate then began to tell Mel and the others Martha's story. They listened in awe as a tale of personal tragedy turned to one of deceit and downright wickedness.

"Martha lived in this house over a hundred years ago. There were five children and she was the eldest." Kate explained. "After her came Freddie, Thomas, Evangeline and Gabriel.

"Things started to go wrong when her brother Freddie fell ill. It turned out to be tuberculosis – a lung disease that people could die of in those days.

"Their parents decided to send Freddie somewhere to try to get better – a place called a sanatorium. It was by the sea and the idea was that the fresh air might be good for his lungs.

"But then the parents grew ill. Their illness was a mystery. The doctors couldn't decide what was wrong. But they grew weaker and weaker every day, and it soon became clear that they could no longer look after themselves, let alone the children. So they advertised for a housekeeper.

"There was only one applicant and Martha's parents couldn't understand why she wanted the job. She was much too good for it. She was a fully qualified governess, who had also turned her hand to nursing in the Crimean War. Not only was she offering to run the house and nurse Martha's parents, but she could give the children their lessons too.

"Martha's parents called her an 'angel of mercy', but behind their backs, this angel ruled with a rod of iron. It was *her* name that the ghostly Martha wrote on my mirror... Cecily Fane.

"Miss Fane wouldn't let the children anywhere near their parents. 'It's a highly contagious disease,' she told them. 'It would break their hearts if they gave it to you.' She wouldn't even let Martha call to her mother through the closed bedroom door.

"Their parents really missed the children and instructed Miss Fane to have a portrait of them painted and hung up in their room. This was done, even though Freddie couldn't be in it, and despite the governess's mutterings of 'money wasted'.

"She began to take charge of life in the house. The weaker Martha's parents grew, the stronger the power Cecily Fane had over them. She seemed so kind and giving, and the more she gave, the more Martha's parents felt they owed her. They trusted her completely and heaped praise on her for everything she did. She had them eating out of her hand. What an actress!

"Martha told me that if I had met her, I would have thought she was a saint, just as Martha's parents had. Anyone would have done. While Martha's parents were alive, nothing was too much trouble. She prepared all their food and drink herself, even down to the special herbal remedies they took. She nursed them day and night, single handed.

"But all along she was just biding her time waiting for them to die, maybe even helping death along a little – who knows what she put in those herbal remedies of hers?

"How Miss Fane must have crowed the day Martha's parents changed their will in her favour. When they were gone, she'd get her hands on this house, 34 Wisteria Gardens, and all the Thackerys' money.

"They made her the legal guardian of the children. It would be down to her to bring them up and make all the decisions about their future. Well, she had already made one decision – as soon as the parents were dead, the children wouldn't have a future! All the hard work and pretence, the sweet smiles and acts of kindness would have paid off, and she could show herself in her true colours.

"And that's exactly what happened. When Martha's parents finally died, she gave up all phoney pretence of caring for the children and started to treat them like dirt. Then she turned the house into an orphanage, taking in waifs and strays from all over Groombridge.

"Even this 'kind' gesture was just another trick in her evil scheme of things. She hoodwinked everyone in Groombridge too. The townspeople fell over themselves to give money to her 'charity'.

"But, when their backs were turned, she treated the orphans as badly as the Thackery children. Every single one of them skivvied for her in return for a mattress on the floor and starvation rations.

"Most of the donations went into her own pocket... along with the money she inherited from Martha's parents. Their last will and testament gave Miss Fane complete control of every last penny that Martha's parents had left..."

Kate paused and pushed her red hair off her forehead. Mel thought she spotted tears in Kate's sad, grey eyes. It was unfamiliar and strangely reassuring to see Kate express some emotion.

"Gabriel was the first to die," said Kate, her voice almost cracking. "Although it was actually the tuberculosis that killed him, Martha told me that Miss Fane did everything to speed up his death.

"She knew how sick he and their brother Tom were. She heard them coughing and saw them wasting away, so she made them work harder than ever. And if they fell asleep when they were supposed to be working – as they very often did towards the end – she would punish them.

"Cecily Fane used to lock 'bad' children in the nursery cupboard, for hours at a time. She knew Gabriel was terrified of the dark, but she was merciless. She would bundle them in, smile a twisted smile and then say 'Lights out!' as she slammed the door shut. Soon Gabriel would begin to cry, his little wasted body shaking with sobs.

"Martha begged Miss Fane to send Gabriel and Tom to the sanatorium where Freddie had gone. But Miss Fane only laughed. That was when she told Martha that Freddie was dead. 'Why pay good money to die, when they can do it here for free?' she had said callously.

"After Gabriel died, Thomas was next... and soon after that it was the turn of Evangeline, Martha's only sister.

"One winter's evening, feeling utterly helpless and alone, Martha confronted her governess. She was leaving, she said. And she wouldn't be back until she had told the world the truth about Cecily Fane.

"Her guardian laughed in her face. What was she going to say? Who was she going to tell? What proof did she have? Martha had no answers to these questions. She had a vague idea the family had a distant relative living in London, but how she could find his address or raise the train fare, she had no idea.

"Cecily Fane called her bluff. She threw open the door, 'What are you waiting for, child?' she demanded. 'Leave now. Tell the world what you want, for all I care. Who will believe you?'

"Staring up into Miss Fane's evil face, Martha knew that she had played right into her hands. Outside, a gale was blowing. Martha's health was failing. She knew that the journey might well defeat her. But she had to try. She couldn't let Cecily Fane win.

"As Martha's ghost spoke, it was as though she was reliving every moment of her final defeat," said Kate. "She twisted her shawl in her bony fingers and her words came in gasps, as if she was fighting for survival all over again." Kate's eyes seemed to burn with the injustice of it.

"She looked at me with such a piercing expression that I couldn't turn away. Her voice had already started to weaken, and as she told me the rest of her sad story, she was already starting to slip away.

"She fled this house and walked and walked in

the gale. Her feet were blistered and her hands were frozen to the bone. She lost her way in the dark and found she could hardly breathe. Then she began to cough and had to rest beside a big boulder on top of Groombridge Heath. It might just as well have been her gravestone." Kate stopped. There was a tremor in her voice.

"Martha sank down at the foot of my bed, reliving that awful night," said Kate. "She put her hands over her head and cowered, as though she was trying to protect herself from the fierce wind and lashing rain.

"And that must have been how she died. As her image began to fade, I felt an overwhelming sense of hopelessness and despair.

"Her last words to me were the same ones she'd first spoken to me in the churchyard. *'Help us! Reveal her for what she was. Avenge the wrongs of the past. Set our souls to rest.'"*

17

Revenge!

"Wow!" said Jason, breaking the silence that followed the closing words of Kate's story. "That was unbelievable, Kate."

Kate shot him a mistrustful glance.

"I mean, it's an amazing story," added Jason hurriedly. "I don't mean I don't believe it. I do." The others nodded their agreement.

"So... it was Martha's ghost who did all those weird things at school?" Matt said slowly.

"Yes," replied Kate.

"Kate," said Mel cautiously. "Did you make Martha's ghost do those things for you? I've... er...

I've read about things like that happening with some people. Sensitives, that's what they're called."

Kate shook her head. "I don't have control over any of this, if that's what you mean. Martha came to me because she wanted my help in some way, and she seems to think she has to fulfil her part of the bargain. This is her way of helping me."

"Helping you?" asked Jason.

"I think so. Whenever I'm really upset or unhappy she seems to do these things," said Kate.

At the mention of Kate being upset, they all looked guiltily to the floor. Few, if any, of them had done much to help Kate stand up to Stevely. They didn't look at one another. If they had, they might have wondered where Stevely was now.

* * * * * * * * * * * * * * * * * * *

Stevely was beginning to despair of ever finding the nursery again. She turned a corner, certain that she would find the door on her left, but there was just an expanse of wall hung with gloomy portraits. Everything seemed so different this time round, but she had only the guttering flame of the candlestick she'd taken from the hall to light her way. No wonder she kept going round in circles.

She took a deep breath. Keep calm! she told herself. She retraced the route they had taken earlier. This was the staircase to the spare room. So that must be the corridor where Tony had disturbed Esmerelda. Here were the back stairs; down one flight, then another, along the corridor. They'd been here before the doorbell rang, so now, if she turned left... surely the nursery was just around the corner. Gripping the brass candlestick determinedly in her trembling hand, she walked on.

* * * * * * * * * * * * * * * * * * *

Downstairs, in the drawing room, the atmosphere was tense and expectant. The gang felt privileged to be let in on Kate's amazing secret, although they were ashamed that it had taken this to make them realize how nasty they'd been to Kate. But right now it wasn't Kate who needed help. It was Martha.

"I don't get it," said Tony, shrugging his shoulders helplessly, "If Martha and Cecily Fane are dead and buried, how can we change anything? It's ancient history."

"No, don't you see?" Mel blurted out, "Cecily Fane's not dead and buried. Her *name* lives on.

96

Everyone still thinks she was a do-gooder, but it's not too late to tell the world what an evil scheming pig she was, behind all that phoney kindness..."

Suddenly the candles guttered. From a distant corner of the room, came a faint rattling noise. A video cassette that had been left on top of the TV was vibrating gently. The vibration became stronger, and the rattle became a clatter.

Soon the whole room seemed to be quaking from floor to ceiling. Pictures swung on their hooks, furniture clattered and knocked and the ghoulish candelabra swayed madly from side to side, throwing hectic shadows about the room. Mel and Matt stared at each other in silent terror.

Then the floorboards started to tremble and creak. Suddenly, a corner of the bearskin rug slid back, revealing a single floorboard that was vibrating so hard that the nails holding it down flew out, like bullets from a gun.

One nail flew straight past Clare, grazing her cheek and drawing blood. A huge splinter of wood narrowly missed Matt's arm. Mel clutched Kate's sleeve, while Clare cowered behind them and the boys stared at each other in blind panic.

There was a horrendous splintering sound as the floorboard finally broke free of the joist beneath it. It flipped up into the air and flew across the room, as if hurled by some superhuman force. Jason ducked as it slammed into the arm chair, and then bounced off again, before coming to rest on the other side of the room. There was silence.

The gang stared in disbelief at the gaping hole in the floor.

* * * * * * * * * * * * * * * * * * *

As Stevely approached the nursery door, she was afraid, but also strangely exhilarated. Ignoring the thumping of her heart, she stretched out and touched the burnished brass door handle. It felt cool in her hand. She took a deep breath, twisted it, and pushed the door open.

Inside, the nursery was surprisingly light. Moonlight streamed in through the bare window, illuminating a scene that appeared not to have been touched for decades, maybe even centuries.

A grand, four-storey doll's house, complete in every detail, stood in one corner and a wooden fort in the other, with lead soldiers abandoned in mid-battle. A window seat was home to a row of dolls whose unblinking eyes stared eerily out of identical white china faces. Nearby a doll's pram with a lacy coverlet stood, empty and forlorn.

Stevely cast nervous glances to either side of her, though she wasn't sure what she expected to see. There was a movement in the corner of the room and Stevely could have sworn she heard faint laughter, quickly stifled. She took a step in the direction of the sound, but then froze as a gentle, rhythmic creaking came from the other direction.

She spun round and saw a huge dappled rocking horse baring its painted teeth at her. Was it her imagination, or had it been rocking all by itself? No, get a grip, she told herself firmly. You're getting carried away. There's no one here. All the same, Stevely couldn't shake off the disturbing feeling that she was being watched. And moments later, she knew why.

Hanging above the mantelpiece was a large oil painting which made Stevely catch her breath. Four children, dressed in old-fashioned clothes, gazed down at her.

Their eyes were sad and watchful and they made Stevely feel strangely guilty. A brave-looking little boy in a jacket and breeches stood on one side of the group. Next to him, the littlest children, a boy and a girl, looked pale and tired. And on the other side, one arm held out protectively toward the little ones, was an older girl. She was the image of the girl in Kate's painting, the one she'd called Martha.

* * * * * * * * * * * * * * * * * *

It was Tony, in the end, who plucked up the courage to tiptoe across the drawing room and peer down into the dusty hole revealed by the floorboard. He lowered what was left of one of the candles into the cavity, almost burning his fingers.

At first sight, it looked disappointing. All he could see under the floor was a dead mouse and a few old hairclips. But just as he was about to give up, the candle flickered and he caught sight of something shining, just beyond his reach.

"Hey! I've found something," he shouted excitedly.

"Careful Tony," said Clare as he lay down flat on the floor and stretched his arm as far as it would go under the boards. He stretched his hand further, further towards the object and at last caught a fold of fabric beneath his fingers. He pulled, gently, holding his breath.

* * * * * * * * * * * * * * * * * *

As Stevely stared up at the painting of the four sad children, she felt Martha's eyes boring into her, just as they had in Kate's picture. It was as though the girl's presence had somehow invaded the room and, try as she might, Stevely couldn't bring herself to look away. Until she heard a faint murmur coming from an enormous built-in cupboard beside the fireplace which stretched from floor to ceiling.

Stevely rested her candlestick on the mantelpiece and started to move in the direction of the sound. As she walked, she became aware of a distant commotion. It sounded and felt as though someone was shifting furniture around downstairs. The noise and vibration got louder and stronger.

Soon the nursery itself was affected. The lead soldiers in the fort slid off the battlements and clattered onto the floor... the lace coverlet on the doll's pram trembled... the oil painting above the mantelpiece shuddered and swayed.

And all the time Stevely could hear the ghost of a giggle coming from the cupboard, as though someone was teasing her, taunting her.

As the shuddering and quaking reached a crescendo, its force snuffed out her candle and at the same time flung open the door of the cupboard, blocking out the moonlight from the window. Suddenly the room was pitch-black, silent and still.

The noise and shuddering had stopped. So had the taunting laughter, although now that Stevely's ears had got used to the quiet, she thought she could hear the faint sigh of someone breathing nearby. Could there be someone in the cupboard? Stevely took a step towards it.

Just then, out of the darkness, something touched her lightly on the cheek. It felt like a thin, cool hand. She shrieked and turned around full circle, her arms stretched out in front of her, as though in a game of blind man's buff.

Stevely panicked and ran, in what she hoped was the direction of the nursery door, but her outstretched arms came in contact with the rough texture of wood panelling. She could tell she was in a confined space and soon became aware of several other bodies, cold and clammy around her. Then she heard the murmuring again. It was very close this time.

"Stevely," the voices seemed to whisper. They were children's voices – high and taunting – sniggering, not with humour, but with malice.

"Stevely!"

Again she felt the lightest of touches on her face, a bony finger poking her in the ribs and the tug of a mischievous little fist around her hair. Then the whispers rose, in a chorus which chilled her blood,

"Lights out!" they chanted, lightly, teasingly – again and again. Stevely felt faint. She sank down into the corner and hid her head in her hands, but still the voices kept up their whispered chant.

"Lights out! Lights out!"

There was a pause. Stevely lifted her head hopefully, wondering if the nightmare was over. Then 'CRASH!' The door of the nursery cupboard slammed shut...

...with Stevely inside it.

18

Letters

"Got it, whatever it is!" said Tony, triumphantly. A cloud of dust billowed out of the hole in the drawing room floor as Tony heaved the heavy object up into the candlelight. It was a big, old-fashioned carpet bag with a brass clasp.

"Here, Kate. I think you should be the one to open it," said Tony, pushing it towards her.

"No," said Kate. "You do it, Mel."

Mel rubbed her thumb over the grimy clasp and gasped as the initials 'C.F' were revealed. "Cecily Fane," she whispered, slowly opening the bag.

Mel recoiled, an instant reflex to shield herself

from the storm of papers that literally burst from the bag. Page after page of paper shot up into the air, whirling, swirling, spinning madly, like a small tornado spiralling out of control.

As the last sheet came to rest on the floor, Mel picked it up gingerly. This wasn't just any old piece of paper. It was a letter. They were all letters.

No one spoke. The air was thick with dust and the musty smell of old paper. Mel leaned forward and peered inside the open carpet bag. Without a word, she tipped it upside down. A bundle of leather-bound books fell onto the floor.

"Take a look at these," said Mel, turning the dusty, yellowed pages of one of the books. "I think we're onto something."

Kate was already scanning one of the letters. "The date on this one is 11th October 1876," she said. "And the signature is C. Fane. But it's a real mess, full of crossings out."

"Perhaps she wrote a neat version later," said Matt, straining to read the spidery writing over Kate's shoulder. "Come to think of it, why else would she have a letter that she'd written to someone else?"

"It's addressed to Josiah Samuel Esquire, Solicitor, Barrow Street, Groombridge," said Kate. "Listen..."

"Dear Sir. Please accept my very humble apologies for the delay in replying to your letter. You will surely appreciate that I have been utterly devastated by the sad deaths of my late employers and only now feel sufficiently composed to attend to matters such as their last will and testament..."

"The lying hound!" spluttered Mel indignantly. She all but killed them herself!"

"Shhh! Let's hear the rest," said Jason.

Kate read on,

"I await your instructions as to a convenient time to sign the relevant... something or other – I can't read that bit... *and so it is my intention to turn 34 Wisteria Gardens into an orphanage. I feel certain that Mr. and Mrs. Thackery would have wanted some good to come from their misfortune and...* there's a bit scribbled out here, something else I can't read, then... *at a later date, I should like to consult you about setting up a charitable foundation to oversee the venture..."*

"What a hypocrite!" exploded Matt. "She makes herself sound so saintly, but if everything Martha said about that Fane hag was true..."

"Just have a look at this," said Mel opening one of the leather-bound books that had fallen out of the carpet bag. "It's her diary." The others crowded round to look at the small, neat spidery writing that filled the old, yellowed pages.

18th October 1876

Dear Diary,

I have to tell someone how perfectly my scheme is taking shape, but there's no one I can trust. People are such fools, therefore I can only commit my darkest thoughts to paper. The way is clear now. My plan is nearing completion. I have but to sign some legal documents and the Thackery money will be mine

The eldest brat continues to irk me with her black looks and insolent air. She sees through my act I fear, but who would take the word of a twelve year old invalid against mine?

She'll be out of the way soon. Despatched, like her wretched brothers and sister and their parents before them.

Who shall remember the Thackerys then? Not a soul! It is I, Cecily Jane who shall be renowned throughout Groombridge for my good works.

Why, if everything goes according to plan, my personal fortune will soon be so great that I may even endow a local school, or hospital and then I shall have everything: all the luxuries that money can buy and immortality as well.

The other pages continued in much the same way. Mel opened a second leather-bound book. Another diary. It seemed Miss Fane had recorded every one of her terrible deeds, day by day. There were cash books as well – all filled with neat columns of small, spidery figures.

Everyone was reading avidly now. And every letter, every diary entry, every figure, was another piece in the jigsaw puzzle that would ruin Cecily Fane's lofty reputation.

"Get this," said Tony, excitedly. "It's a copy of a letter she sent to the leaders of Groombridge Parish Council. It's really creepy..."

Everyone was silent as Tony read the words that Cecily Fane had written well over a century ago.

"It is with great humility and gratitude that I acknowledge your gift to the Cecily Fane Foundation of four hundred pounds. I should like to add it to funds that I have been setting aside for a new and ambitious project of a charitable nature. Please forgive me for not revealing the details of this scheme yet, but for business reasons, I believe it prudent to keep my counsel until my plans are nearer fruition..."

"I bet I know what that turned out to be," put in Jason.

"What?" asked Clare.

"Our school. Some act of charity that was! I wish

she'd just pocketed the cash."

"Well according to this," said Matt, waving a scrap of paper in the air, "she was pocketing plenty of it as well. Look..."

DEAR C,
 JUST DROPING YOUS A LINE TO LET YOU
KNOW I RECIEVED THE LATEST CHECK AND
I'VE BUNGED IT WELL OUT OF HARMS WAY,
SAME AS THE OTHERS. YOU'VE BUILT UP
QUITE A TIDY SUM BY NOW AND I'M SURE
THEIR'S PLENTY MORE TO COME, NOT
FORGETTING MY CUT, EH?
 MOTHER SENDS HER BEST REGARDS,
B.F.

"Looks like she had an accomplice," said Matt.

"With the initials B.F," Jason added. "What about *mother sends her best regards*? Sounds like another dodgy member of the Fane clan to me."

"Cecily was obviously the brains of the family then," joked Mel.

But Clare interrupted her, "Wait a minute, look at this." She was holding a letter addressed to Miss Cecily Fane. The words on it had been written on an old-fashioned typewriter. The others gathered round and read in silence.

11th November 1910

Dear Madam,

Forgive me for writing to you without ever having made your acquaintance. This may come as a surprise to you, but my name is Frederick Thackery. I am the sole surviving member of the Thackery family.

As you will doubtless recall, the rest of my family died many years ago of a terrible disease. At that time, I was in a sanatorium, making a slow recovery when, owing to what I can only suppose was an administrative error, my fees were stopped abruptly. I was transferred to the local Workhouse, a sorry place which was full of the sick, the old and the weak. As you may imagine, my health worsened rapidly, but against all the odds I survived.

In time, I came to hear of you and your enormous kindness to my family. I wanted to thank you many times, but I always shied away. I had no wish to return to 34 Wisteria Gardens. It had too many unhappy associations for me.

But as time has gone on, my circumstances have changed. I am now a married man with a family of my own. Although my childhood home still brings back some sad memories, maturity has found my thoughts turning more and more to Groombridge and to 34 Wisteria Gardens in particular. I hope you will not think me impertinent if I enquire whether you have ever thought of selling the property?

I look forward to your reply and hope that you will consider my offer to purchase the property a genuine one.

Yours respectfully,

Frederick T. Thackery

Frederick T. Thackery

"That explains it," exclaimed Kate, snatching the letter out of Clare's hands, in her excitement. "Cecily Fane told Martha that Freddie died in the sanatorium. But he didn't. He lived! He was my great-great grandfather."

"I bet that was no administrative error," Tony fumed. "Miss Fane probably stopped the payments as soon as the Thackery parents died. She must have known he'd end up in the workhouse. She as good as signed his death warrant..."

"Except that he survived," Clare grinned. "I wonder what Cecily Fane did when she got that letter. She must have been furious!"

"Scared, more like," said Matt.

Mel was thumbing through Cecily Fane's diaries from the same period. "Here we are," said Mel. "This is what she wrote on 12th November 1910..."

"He's alive. I was shocked to discover it, and just a little afraid. But what a fool he appears to be. As a grown man, this last remaining Thackery thinks me a saint, yet I do the devil's work! He could have said I ruined his life and family, but he writes in praise of me."

"What about this," said Kate, who had unearthed a copy of a letter from Cecily Fane to Freddie Thackery. "Even after all she'd done, she still couldn't resist putting one over on poor Freddie all those years later. Look..."

34 Wisteria Gardens, East Groombridge

11th January 1911

Dear Mr. Thackery,

After due consideration, I have finally made up my mind. In view of my advanced years, I am prepared to accept your offer to purchase 34 Wisteria Gardens. However, I must stress that I feel it is only fair to consider the future of the foundation in settling a purchase price.

As you will know, house values have gone up considerably over the last few years and East Groombridge is a most select area, and very desirable in every way.

I am sure we will be able to agree upon an acceptable figure, knowing how very keen you are to move back into your family home.

I look forward to hearing from you. An early reply would be appreciated as I have had a number of very generous offers for the property already, and I should hate you to be disappointed.

Yours Sincerely,

Cecily Fane

"What a cheek!" gasped Matt, "making Freddie pay through the nose for a house that should have been his by rights all along!"

"Yes. By that stage, Cecily Fane must have thought she could get away with *anything*," agreed Jason.

"She could," said Mel with a shrug. "She *did*."

"Until now," added Kate.

19

Name calling

It was only when they had finished looking through the letters and diaries that the others finally noticed that Stevely was missing and went off in search of her.

They eventually found her in the nursery cupboard. She seemed almost delirious.

"Leave me alone, leave me alone!" she cried, struggling with her rescuers. "No, no, please don't put the lights out! Please! I'm frightened of the dark..."

"She's finally flipped," said Jason.

He tried to make her look at him, but she

crouched in a huddled heap in the corner of the cupboard and wouldn't come out. Her eyes were strangely vacant.

"Stevely, it's me, Jason. We're all here," he said. "Your friends."

"She's terrified of something," said Clare.

"They... they're in here," Stevely shuddered. "Children. They're so cold... so very cold... clammy ... awful. They t-t-t-tricked me. I couldn't see. I must have fainted..."

Kate and Mel looked at each other.

Stevely suddenly stood up and lurched out of the cupboard, straight into Kate's outstretched arms. "I'm sorry, Kate. I'm sorry," she mumbled.

"It's over," said Kate, taking Stevely's hand, as she led them out of the forbidden room. "Let's put it all in the past."

Stevely let herself be led towards the brightly lit doorway. As she passed the fireplace, she glanced at the portrait over the mantelpiece. Something drew her eyes to the picture of the four children. Something was different... The children were standing as they had been before, in exactly the same places, in exactly the same clothes. Their poses were identical, but their expressions had changed.

Instead of the sad, reproachful stares they had

worn before, the children were smirking mischievously, as though they were sharing a private joke.

Stevely knew then, beyond any doubt, that these were the children who had enticed her into the cupboard. Theirs were the clammy hands that had teased and tormented her in the dark. She stumbled, put a hand to her forehead and started to mutter almost to herself.

She seemed about to pass out again, but Kate was holding her, and together she and Mel helped Stevely from the room.

"So what do we do now?" said Mel, once they had all settled back down in the drawing room. The power had come back on and the candles had been extinguished. Suddenly 34 Wisteria Gardens didn't seem so frightening any more.

"The diaries are enough to show that Cecily Fane was a thief and a liar," she said, "but what can we do with them?"

It was Kate who came up with the solution. "Let's send them to the local newspaper," she said.

"Great idea," said Matt. "The *Groombridge Times* loves raking up old scandals. I'm sure they'll make the most of it."

He was right. A few weeks later, the whole story

ran on pages four and five of the *Groombridge Times* under the banner headline:

LOCAL BENEFACTOR DISGRACED

The article showed extracts from Cecily Fane's diaries along with copies of old photographs and even a picture of 34 Wisteria Gardens when it first opened as an orphanage.

Under the subheading '**Letters from the grave**' they reproduced a number of Miss Fane's 'humble' letters next to those from the mysterious 'B.F'. The newspaper named him as her brother, Bartholomew Fane. Over the years, he helped his sister to conceal her ill-gotten gains, but in 1911, he disappeared in mysterious circumstances, and was never seen again.

The newspaper story said nothing about *how* these diaries or letters had come to light. Kate and the others hadn't told anyone else about Martha and the amazing supernatural events that had led up to the discovery. Who would believe them anyway? The article revealed one or two more things they hadn't known, but nothing that came as any surprise.

Miss Fane had died in 1919 at a ripe old age, apparently untroubled by her life of treachery and fraud. She had sold the house – 34 Wisteria Gardens – to Freddie, for a vast amount of money, which she had invested in another of her so called charitable schemes. By the time she died, she must have been a very wealthy woman, although her fortune was never found.

One final shock came during the head teacher's speech on the last day of term at Cecily Fane High. "And so, students, parents, friends," her voice boomed out, filling the packed school hall. "This is the last assembly we shall hold as Cecily Fane High School. We are proud of our heritage. Proud of our achievements, but alas, can no longer be proud of the name Cecily Fane."

A murmur went around the hall. Stevely, Mel and Kate all looked at each other. What was coming next?

"Next term we shall gather together again in the same school buildings, with the same eagerness and thirst for knowledge..." Stevely shot Mel a look of humorous disbelief. "But when the new term begins, so will a new chapter in the history of our school. From then on, we shall be known as Groombridge High School!"

There was a spontaneous burst of applause, then the school orchestra struck up a military march and everyone started to file slowly out of the hall.

Mel took her two friends by the arm. Stevely smiled at Kate, Kate winked at Stevely. Then the three girls walked out onto the playground, into the bright, winter sunshine.

"She's gone," said Kate.

"Who?" asked Mel and Stevely together.

"Martha," said Kate. "I can't feel her presence any more. She must be happy. I'm alone at last."

"Not quite," smiled Stevely. "You've got us, remember."

"Come on," said Mel. "It's the *holidays*!"